DREAM

MADAGASCAR™

Meet ... the animals from

Alex, Marty, Melman and Gloria are friends. They live in New York Zoo.

I'm King Julien. I'm a lemur. I can dance and sing.
King Julien
We are lemurs. We live with King Julien in Madagascar.
The lemurs
We are fossa. We like lemurs for dinner.
The fossa
Before you read ...
What do you think? In this story, who is good? Who is bad?

New Words

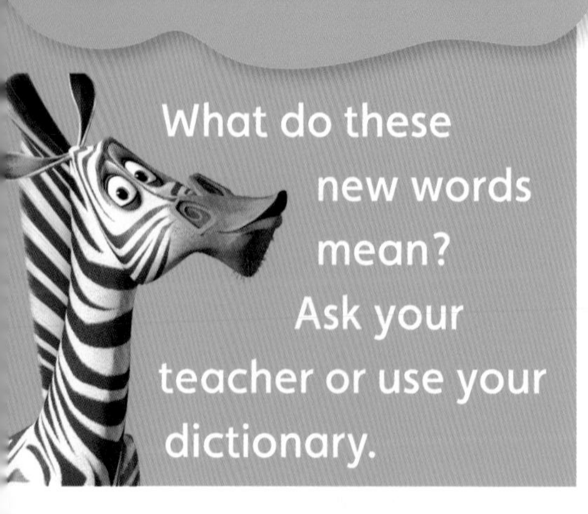

box

What's in the **box**?

beautiful

The girl is **beautiful**.

catch

boat

It's a white **boat**.

fish

Look at the **fish**!

meat

Do you like **meat**?

wild

The animals are in the **wild**.

medicine

This is **medicine**.

zoo

The animals are in the **zoo**.

push

She's **pushing** her brother.

'Happy Birthday!'

CHAPTER 1
'The zoo is our home!'

It is Marty the zebra's birthday.

'Happy Birthday!' say his friends.

But Marty is not happy. 'I'm ten years old and I don't want to be in this zoo. Come to the wild with me!' he says.

'The wild?' laughs Alex the lion. 'But everyone in New York loves me!'

'And there's no medicine in the wild!' says Melman the giraffe.

'The zoo is our home!' says Gloria the hippo.

That night, Marty runs away from the zoo.

'Oh no!' says Alex. 'Where is he?'

Alex, Gloria and Melman go into town. They see Marty.

'Come home to the zoo!' they say.

Suddenly there are men in front of them and men behind them.

'Hello, everyone!' says Alex.

The men do not say hello. They catch the animals.

Alex opens his eyes. It is dark.
'Where am I?' he asks.
'In a box,' says Gloria. 'We're on a boat.'
'We're going to a new zoo,' says Melman.
'I don't want a new zoo!' says Alex.

Alex is angry with Marty. He pushes Marty's box. Then Marty pushes Alex's box. They push the boxes off the boat.

CHAPTER 2
In the wild

The boxes with the four friends are in the sea. They go to Madagascar.

'This isn't a zoo,' says Alex. 'This is the wild!'

'Let's go and see!' says Marty.

They see some lemurs. King Julien is singing and dancing.

Suddenly the lemurs shout, 'Fossa! Run!'

The fossa like lemurs for dinner. But the fossa see Alex and run away.

'Can we go home now?' Alex asks that night.

'No, we can't!' says Marty. 'The wild is cool!'

He makes dinner for his friends.

'Thanks, Marty! This is nice,' say Melman and Gloria.

'It's green!' says Alex. 'I can't eat this.'

Madagascar is beautiful. The zoo animals are happy, but Alex is very hungry.

Suddenly Alex's eyes do not see lemurs and friends – they see meat.

'RAAAAHHH!' he shouts.

Alex runs after Marty. He wants Marty for dinner.

'What are you doing?' shouts Marty.

Alex stops.
'Oh no!' says Alex. 'Marty is my friend!'
Alex is very sad and he goes away.

CHAPTER 3
The boat

A boat comes to Madagascar. Marty, Melman and Gloria are very happy. Marty looks for Alex.

'Stop!' shout Melman and Gloria. 'Alex wants you for dinner!'

But Marty does not listen.

Marty sees Alex

'There's a boat,' says Marty. 'We can go home!'

'Go away!' says Alex. 'We can't be friends.'

Suddenly there are fossa behind Marty. He runs, but there are fossa in front of him too.

'Oh no!' he shouts.

Melman and Gloria come. The three friends run, but the fossa are quick.

'What can we do now?' asks Melman.

Then they see Alex.

'Go away, please!' Alex says to the fossa. 'The zoo animals are *my* dinner!'

The fossa don't go away.

'RAAAAHHH!' shouts Alex.

The fossa run away.

'RAAAAHHH!' shouts Alex again.

'Oh no!' says Marty. 'Alex is hungry!' He closes his eyes.

Suddenly Alex stops.

'Can we go to the boat now?' he says.

'No, we can't!' laughs Marty. 'We have something for you.'

The lemurs make fish for Alex.
'This is nice!' he says. 'Thank you!'

The zoo animals go to the boat.
'Goodbye!' they shout.
'Goodbye!' shout King Julien and the lemurs.
'Can we go home now?' says Alex.
But the boat does not start.
'No, we can't!' says Marty.
'OH NOOOOO!' say the animals.

THE END

THE ISLAND OF MADAGASCAR

Madagascar is an island in the Indian Ocean. Let's read about some of the animals there.

Lemurs

Lemurs live in trees. They eat plants and small animals. **Aye-ayes** are lemurs with big ears and long hands. They sleep in the day and eat at night.

Ring-tailed lemurs sleep at night. They live in groups. What colour are their tails?

Fossa

Fossa live under trees, and they sometimes go up trees too. They eat lemurs. Is this fossa hungry?

Did you know ...?

- Madagascar is home to 5% of the world's plant and animal groups.
- 80% of the plants and animals in Madagascar live only there.

Chameleons

This is a **panther chameleon**. Angry panther chameleons are red and yellow. Cold panther chameleons are a dark colour. Is this chameleon cold or angry?

What do these words mean? Find out.

island plant world only group

After you read

1 Match the sentences and the animals.

a) It's his birthday.
b) They live in a zoo.
c) He is Marty's friend.
d) He is a lemur.
e) They eat lemurs.

i) King Julien
ii) Marty
iii) the fossa
iv) Melman and Gloria
v) Alex

2 Put the sentences in order. Write 1–8.

a) The zoo animals are in Madagascar. ☐
b) King Julien says 'Goodbye!' to the animals. ☐
c) The animals say 'Happy Birthday!' to Marty. [1]
d) Marty runs away from the zoo. ☐
e) The boat does not start. ☐
f) Alex wants Marty for dinner. ☐
g) The animals are in boxes on a boat. ☐
h) The animals see King Julien. ☐

Where's the popcorn?
Look in your book.
Can you find it?

Puzzle time!

1 Where do the boats go? Write sentences.

Example: Boat 1 goes to the bus.

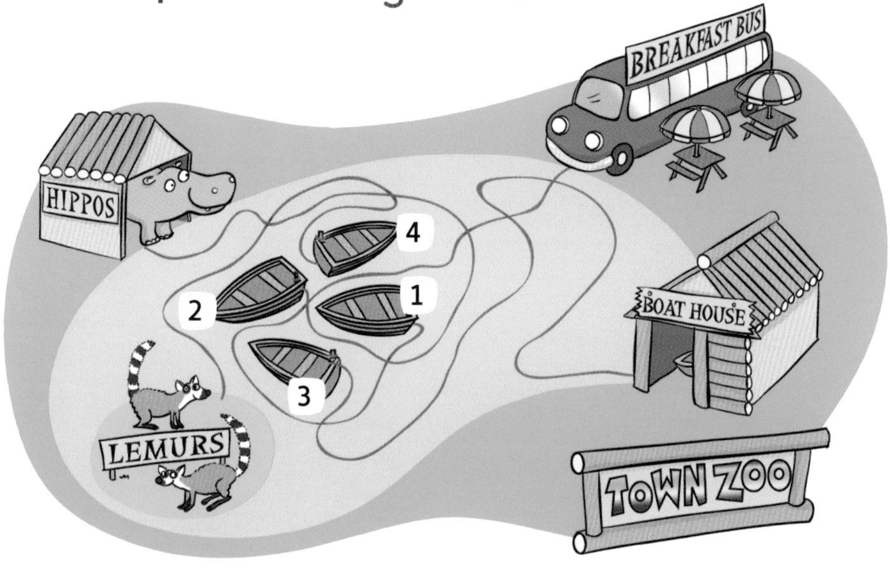

2 Write the animal's name on its box.

fish ~~zebra~~ hippo lemur giraffe

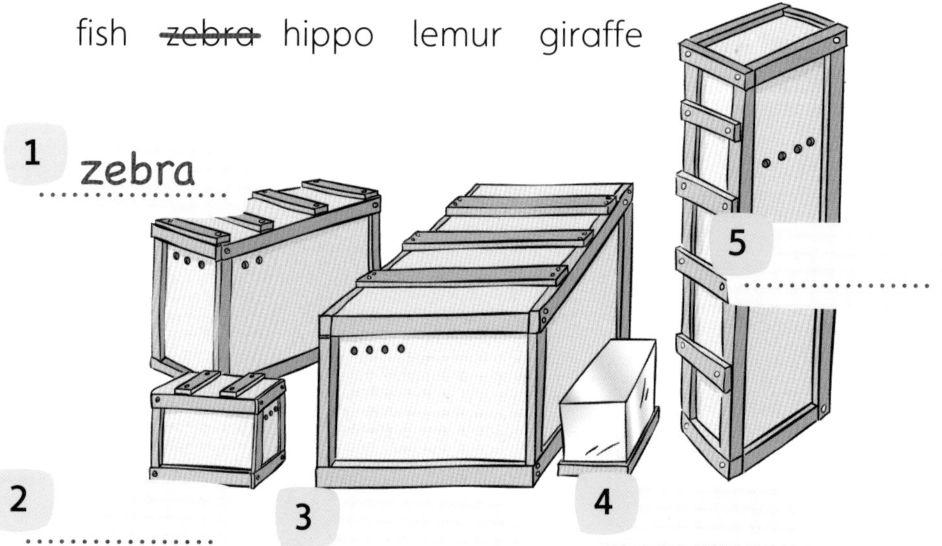

3 What is the lemur doing? Match the words and the pictures.

a) He's laughing.

b) He's singing.

c) He's pushing.

d) He's dancing.

e) He's eating.

4 Look at the pictures and do the crossword.

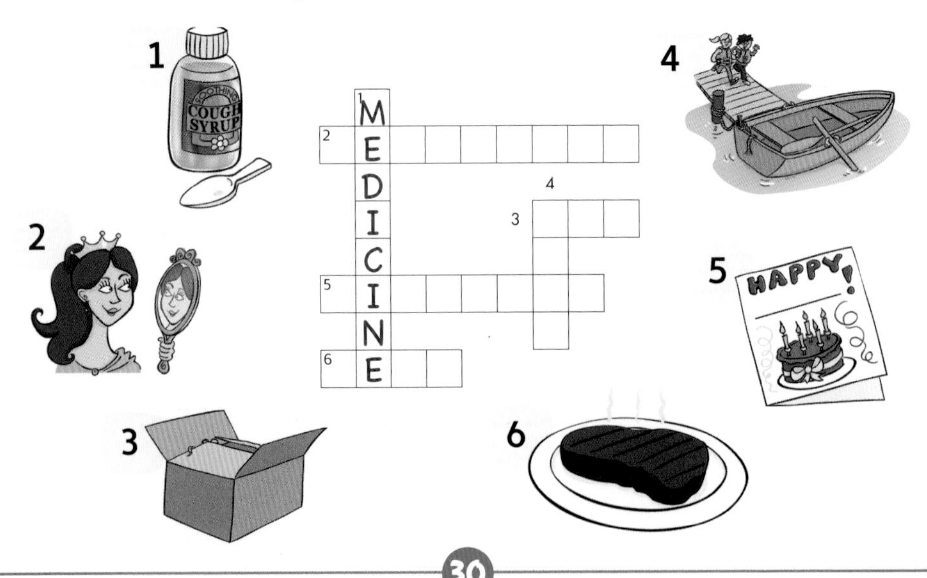

Imagine ...

Work with two friends.
Act out the scenes.

A

Alex and Melman: Happy Birthday, Marty!

Marty: I'm ten years old and I don't want to be in this zoo.

Alex: But everyone in New York loves me!

Melman: And there's no medicine in the wild!

B

Alex: Where am I?

Gloria: In a box. We're on a boat.

Melman: We're going to a new zoo.

Alex: I don't want a new zoo!

C

Alex: Can we go home now?

Marty: No, we can't! The wild is cool!

Gloria: Thanks, Marty! This is nice!

Alex: It's green! I can't eat this.

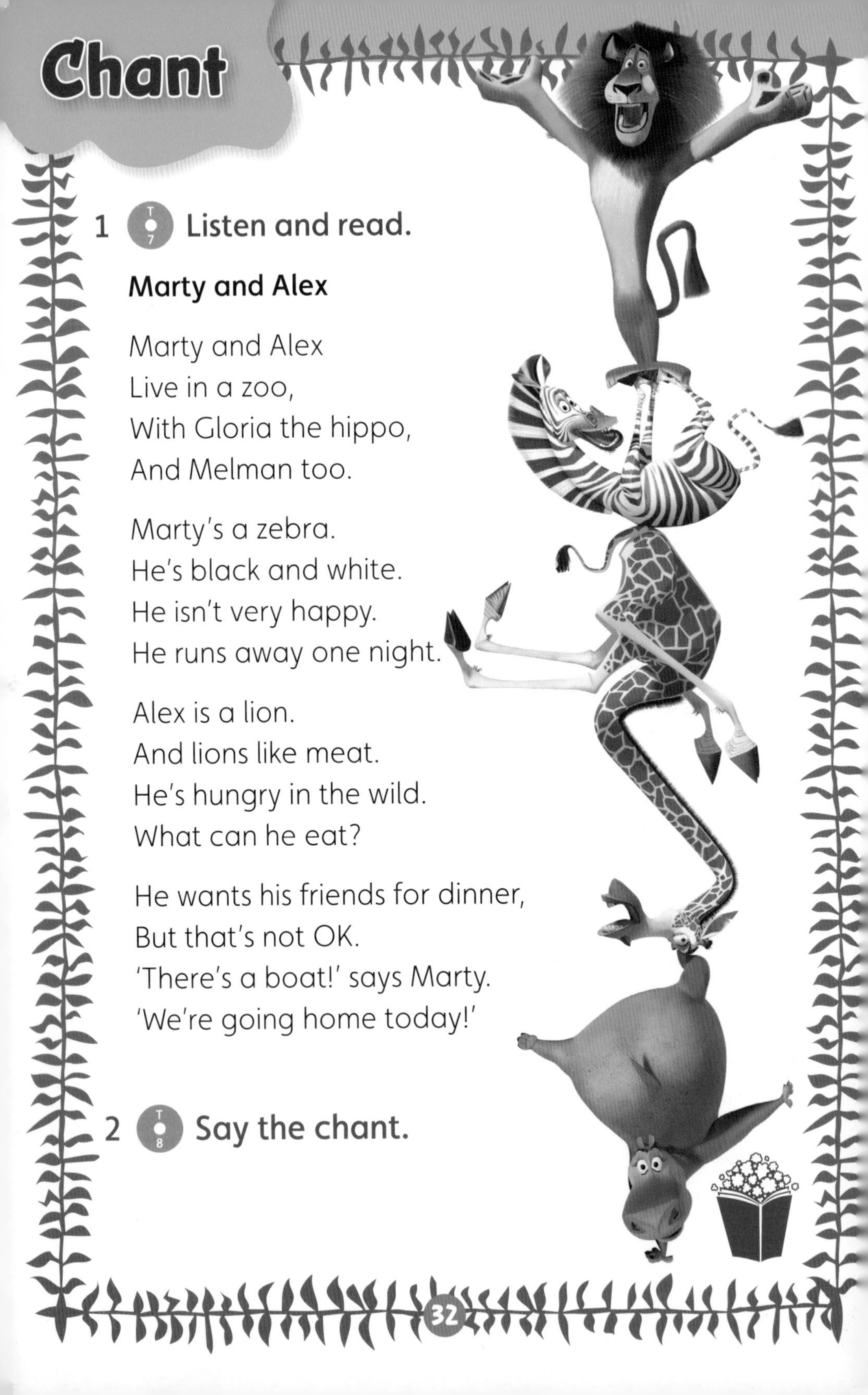

Chant

1 T7 **Listen and read.**

Marty and Alex

Marty and Alex
Live in a zoo,
With Gloria the hippo,
And Melman too.

Marty's a zebra.
He's black and white.
He isn't very happy.
He runs away one night.

Alex is a lion.
And lions like meat.
He's hungry in the wild.
What can he eat?

He wants his friends for dinner,
But that's not OK.
'There's a boat!' says Marty.
'We're going home today!'

2 T8 **Say the chant.**